Praise for Storyshares

"One of the brightest innovators and game-changers in the education industry."
— Forbes

"Your success in applying research-validated practices to promote literacy serves as a valuable model for other organizations seeking to create evidence-based literacy programs."
— Library of Congress

"We need powerful social and educational innovation, and Storyshares is breaking new ground. The organization addresses critical problems facing our students and teachers. I am excited about the strategies it brings to the collective work of making sure every student has an equal chance in life."
— Teach For America

"It's the perfect idea. There's really nothing like this. I mean, wow, this will be a wonderful experience for young people."
— Andrea Davis Pinkney, Executive Director, Scholastic

"Reading for meaning opens opportunities for a lifetime of learning. Providing emerging readers with engaging texts that are designed to offer both challenges and support for each individual will improve their lives for years to come. Storyshares is a wonderful start."
— David Rose, Co-founder of CAST & UDL

Jorge

Storyshares presents

Published by Storyshares, LLC

Storyshares
Storyshares, LLC
24 N. Bryn Mawr Avenue #340
Bryn Mawr, Pennsylvania 19010-3304
www.storyshares.org

Inspiring reading with a new kind of book.

Interest Level: High School
Grade Level Equivalent: 3.7

ISBN 9781642614916
Book design by Saskia Globig

JORGE

A PEOPLE MOVERS STORY

Brian Kirchner

Storyshares

CONTENTS

ONE
I Feel Good!

I nodded to Kenji from across the stage. He was wailing away on his bass, but he nodded back. Our drummer Yusuf's thundering backbeat was winding up to a climax. X, our lead singer, was screeching out a banshee wail.

Kenji and I jumped up onto the drummer riser, which was about three feet off the stage. We leapt off it in unison, our guitars held high over our heads. At the same moment, the stage lights started strobing in six different colors.

As Kenji and I flew through the air, Yusuf executed a perfect triplet roll. He built up to a long rattle with his splash cymbals. X dropped to his knees. He turned his face up to the rafters, squeezed his eyes shut, and held the microphone near his mouth. He held that same banshee note. My bassist and I landed on either side of X.

I gunned a final power E-chord on my Fender Strat. You could barely hear it because the crowd in the Royal Oak Music Theater was going insane. I mean C-R-A-Z-Y. Every single person in the place was on their feet and screaming. My heart pounded like I'd just run a marathon. I thought that I'd lost a gallon of water in sweat over the course of our hour-long set.

X leapt to his feet, impressively unfolding his lanky, six-foot frame in the blink of an eye. His huge, basketball-sized Afro floated around his head. He was grinning from ear to ear. So was Kenji. We stared at each other. I realized I was grinning too. I was grinning so hard my face hurt.

I spun around and looked at Yusuf. He was standing behind his kit, sticks raised high in the air. On his head was his trademark straw cowboy hat. It had an American flag bandanna wrapped around the crown and a ragged hole in the side. That hole was the result of an encounter with a nasty neighborhood knucklehead a couple of years back. It was right after Yusuf and his family moved to America from Syria.

The crowd was going berserk. The yelling soon turned into a chant: "MORE! MORE! MORE! MORE!" The sound filled the old music hall like an explosion of audio confetti.

Yusuf bounded out from around his kit. He joined the rest of us at the front of the stage. We all lined up and draped our arms over each other's shoulders. We took a deep, dramatic bow. Yusuf whipped his hat off just in time to avoid losing it into the crowd.

"MORE! MORE! MORE! MORE!" The chant kept going, and we bowed again. Then we all looked at each other. There was no need to say anything (not that we would have been able to hear each other, anyway). Each of us knew what the others were thinking.

As if on cue, the crowd's chant morphed into, "I FEEL GOOD! I FEEL GOOD! I FEEL GOOD!"

"Yeah, baby, we know what you want!" X shouted into his mic. "That's right! We hear you! The People Movers hear you!"

The chant dissolved into wild screaming again.

We got back into place. Yusuf ran behind his kit. He rolled off a couple of quick licks and a cymbal crash. Kenji and I retreated to opposite sides of the stage. X stayed at the front. When he saw we were ready, he counted off, "ONE! TWO! ONETWO-THREEFOUR!!"

We swung into our signature tune. It was a cover of James Brown's "I Feel Good." X did the Godfather of Soul justice not only with his singing but with his moves. We were giving the people what they wanted. We were all right in time, and let me tell you, it felt freaking amazing.

But the best and craziest part came towards the end of the song. We'd decided to do a little experimenting with pyrotechnics. We used a flashpot X had bought from a theatrical supply company.

The little device was planted behind Yusuf's drum riser. Yusuf had a remote-control pedal that he would press at a certain point in the song.

And the thing worked. In fact, that's an understatement. Flames shot up behind Yusuf. Smoke billowed up so thick that it enveloped Yusuf, his drums, and a moment later, the rest of the stage.

The crowd loved it. Us, not so much. It took twenty minutes for us to stop coughing. Our eyes watered for an hour afterward. And the people who ran St. Andrews... Let's just say we were invited to leave and not come back for a very long time.

We made the local paper the next day. The front-page headline said, "Local Band is Smokin' Hot!"

TWO
Fun with Magnesium

You're probably wondering who I am. I'm Carlos Villareal. I'm seventeen, and I'm in a band called the People Movers. I play lead guitar, Kenji Omura is on bass, Yusuf Karout is on drums, and Xavier Maplethorpe is on lead vocals (everyone just calls him X).

We live in Rochester, Michigan. It's a little way north of Detroit.

We started out just playing around in my garage back when we were high school freshmen. Things have gotten more serious now.

We actually make a little bit of money from our music. They say money ruins everything, but so far, it's a lot better than delivering pizza or washing dishes.

Why the name People Movers? It started as kind of a joke, really.

Back when we started the band, while we were brainstorming names, X made a crack about Detroit's People Mover. It's an elevated train that makes a pretty useless little circle around a few downtown attractions. X said that the People Mover didn't move any people. He said they should call it the Ghost Train instead. Then I said that our band made people move (at least we hoped it would), so maybe we should take the People Mover name.

Everyone had laughed... at first. But the more we brainstormed, the more it made sense. We just added the *s* since there were four of us. We play funk and rhythm and blues. Music that makes people get up and move. You feel me?

The next day, we were all still riding on the adrenaline from the Royal Oak show. We were hanging out in my garage on Alice Street in Rochester. The garage door was open. Bright summer sunlight streamed in, along with muggy heat. Normally, we'd be jamming, since my garage was our practice space. But today, X was showing us the wonders of magnesium.

When I say magnesium, I don't mean the stuff you get in nutrition pills. Well, it is the same, but the stuff we had was pure. In the pills, magnesium is combined with other stuff so you can't see it for what it really is.

We all stood around a small workbench against one wall of the garage. X had a thick, steel canister with a small pile of dull gray metal shavings in it. He placed the canister on the bench. He held one of those long lighters you use for fireplaces and barbeques, the kind with a little trigger on it.

"You sure this is safe?" I asked, thinking of all our band gear piled around us.

"No worries, C-man," X said. "The thickness of the can is exactly ten percent more than it needs to be to absorb the heat output of ten grams of burning magnesium."

"You figured that out, huh?"

"'Course I did. I don't wanna burn your house down. Now let's get on with the demo. I think this stuff will make a righteous stage effect if we learn how to use it right."

Kenji, Yusuf, and I all took a step back from

the bench. X flicked the flame on and touched it to the metal shavings.

The reaction was instantaneous. A brilliant miniature fireball of pure white heat flared inside the can, lighting up everything within five feet of it. Wisps of smoke poured from the can, and the whole thing made a loud hissing sound. I could feel warmth from the can even from several steps away.

As we watched, the steel walls of the can began to turn a dull red.

"Uh, dude," I said. "That can's going to melt."

"No, it ain't," said X, smiling.

The can turned bright crimson. The hissing, white-hot fireball continued to blaze inside it.

"You have a fire extinguisher, right?" Yusuf asked me.

I nodded, jerking my thumb at the fat, red cylinder hanging just inside the garage door. I kept my eyes on the can, waiting for it to vaporize and release a raging chemical inferno. But that didn't happen. Just as the metal of the can was beginning to warp, the light died down and sputtered out. The can's glow faded. The heat dissipated.

X grabbed a pair of barbecue tongs from the wall of the garage and picked up the can. He showed it to us. It was blackened and bent but intact. The magnesium itself was gone except for a thin layer of black ash on the bottom of the can.

"See? Cool, right?"

"Where'd you get this stuff?" Kenji asked.

"Amazon."

I started to laugh, then realized he was serious.

"Magnesium is awesome," Yusuf said. "We should use it in our next show."

"Skins man has spoken!" said X, fist bumping our drummer. Yusuf's cell phone rang.

"Hi, *Yummu*," he said, using the Arabic word for mom. "What's going on?"

Whatever she said next made Yusuf frown. She spoke for about thirty seconds. Then Yusuf said, "Okay, I'll be there in a few minutes." Then he ended the call.

"What was that about?" Kenji said.

"Kind of hard to explain," he replied. "There's a kid at our apartment. He's a refugee from El Salvador. He just got there."

"Uh, dude, why is there a Central American kid at your apartment?" I asked.

Instead of giving a direct answer, Yusuf just said, "Because it's Allah's will. Come on. Let's go over there."

THREE

Underground Railroad

If you've never been lucky enough to spend time in the home of a family from the Middle East, then it's hard for me to describe the combination of aromas that hit me as I entered Yusuf's house. I had been in the Karouts' apartment many times, but the smells never failed to spin my head around. Today, I smelled a delicious mix of spices, garlic, incense, and five or six other scents I couldn't identify.

"*Yummu!*" called Yusuf, walking toward the kitchen. "Mom! Who's that—oh, hi, *Yabba*. Pop, where's

Mom? She said a kid showed up a while ago."

Yusuf stood just inside the kitchen. We all gathered behind him. Yusuf's father, a slight, balding man with wiry arms and intense, intelligent eyes, was preparing a small meal. He smiled when he saw us.

"*Al-salaam alaykum*, boys," he said. He bowed slightly and placed his right hand over his heart. We all responded with "*Wa alaykum al-salaam*, Mr. Karout," and returned the gesture. Yusuf had taught us the traditional Muslim greeting shortly after joining our band.

Mr. Karout's smile faded. "Yes, Yusuf. There is a child here, a refugee from El Salvador. He is with your mother in your bedroom. He doesn't speak any English, only Spanish. He is very frightened. Sayeed brought him from Toledo. Very young, perhaps only seven years old."

Mr. Karout shook his head sadly. "This separation of families policy... *Na'outh bi Allah*! Allah protect us!"

"Maybe you should tell my friends about what we've been doing," said Yusuf.

Mr. Karout nodded. "We assist refugees who are trying to get into Canada. Others like us, such as our good friend Sayeed El-Saghir in Toledo, bring them to us. Then we help them with the final step in their journey. Being so close to the Canadian border here makes us an ideal last stop."

"You mean, you guys have been running, like, an Underground Railroad for refugee kids?" I said.

Mr. Karout looked me with a puzzled expression. "Underground—?"

"Slaves, *Yabba*," explained Yusuf. "In the nineteenth century in America, when people would help slaves escape to freedom, they called it the Underground Railroad."

Mr. Karout nodded thoughtfully. "Yes, something like that."

"Totally cool," said X. "You guys are legit heroes, Mr. K."

Yusuf's father continued. "No, we are just ordinary people. The Prophet Mohammad, peace be upon him, teaches us in the Holy Quran that it is the duty of every Muslim to extend hospitality to all guests, friends and strangers alike.

"This is especially true of those who are in extreme need, like we were when we first came to America. The three of you," he said, looking at Kenji, X, and me in turn, "extended such hospitality to us. This is something for which I give great thanks to Allah every day."

"Aw, Mr. K. We were just tryin' to do the right thing," said X.

Mr. Karout nodded. "Yes. It seems very straightforward, doesn't it? But how much of the trouble in the world is caused by those who choose not to do the right thing? You helped us, even though you didn't know us. Even though it might have resulted in trouble for yourselves from that bully."

Mr. Karout was talking about the summer we met Yusuf and his family. A local fool by the name of Derek Bodley had decided he didn't like having a Syrian family in the neighborhood. He had tried to frame Yusuf for some ugly graffiti spray-painted on the Bodley garage door.

Kenji, X, and I had proven that Bodley was the one behind it.

Because of the Make America Safe Again Act (perpetrated by the same idiots in Washington who were responsible for the current crisis of refugee kids being separated from their parents), the Karouts would have been deported if Yusuf had taken the blame for the graffiti. One strike and you're out, baby. Disgusting.

Bodley had also been the one who tore the hole in Yusuf's straw hat. I asked Yusuf why he never fixed the hole or got rid of the hat. His answer had been short and right on: "Because I always want to remember how close my family came to losing everything." My man Yusuf is a top-notch drummer and the bravest dude I know.

"Because of this enjoinment from the Prophet, and because we were refugees once, we are helping the children torn from their parents in any way we can. We take them in, we feed them, we hide them if necessary. And most of all, we show them kindness," Mr. Karout explained. "This is what they need most of all."

FOUR
Mara Salvatrucha

"Can we see the kid, *Yabba*?" asked Yusuf.

"Yes. Come this way." Mr. Karout gestured for us to follow him.

We trooped out of the kitchen and into a short hall with three other doors off of it. Only one was open. Mr. Karout stepped through that door. We followed him.

The door led to a tiny bedroom that was clearly Yusuf's. The décor was a mix of Syrian traditional and modern American rock, if you can picture that.

On the neatly made single bed, sat Mrs. Karout. She was a short, round-faced woman. Her head was wrapped in a bright-blue hijab.

Next to Mrs. Karout was the boy. He wasn't crying, but his face was stained with tears. He was wrapped in a big, red-and-blue beach towel.

He was skinny—that was my first impression. His brown face was all angles and corners. His collarbones stuck out above the edge of the towel. His dark-brown hair was a tangled riot. An angry lightning bolt shaped scar slashed across one cheek. I wondered how he got it.

His wide, brown eyes looked from one of us to another, back and forth, half curious and half scared. In his hand was a glass of milk. I noticed the glass shaking slightly.

"Hello, Carlos, Kenji, and X," said Mrs. Karout softly. She bowed her head slightly to each of us. "Please meet our guest. His name is Jorge."

"Hey, little brother," said X, taking Mrs. Karout's cue and speaking softly. He squatted, folding his gangly frame down to manageable size. He looked into the kid's eyes. "How you doin', my man?"

The boy stared back at X. His eyes took in our lead singer's Afro. I wondered if he'd ever seen someone with an Afro before. It didn't seem like it, the way he was checking out X's monster example of one.

"I don't think he speaks any English," said Mrs. Karout.

X nodded. "Right on, right on. Only Spanish?"

"I think so. That's all he's spoken with me. Not that he's said much. Just his name and a few other words. I don't speak the language, unfortunately." She looked at me hopefully.

"Sorry, Mrs. K, all I know is 'que pasa' and 'yo quiero.' That means Taco Bell," I said. I hated to disappoint her, but it was the truth.

"I know Spanish," said Kenji.

We all looked at him in surprise.

"Since when, man?" said X.

Kenji looked peeved. "Since I learned it from a CD during summer camp when I was in sixth grade."

X shrugged. "Kenji Omura, United Nations translator, ladies and gentlemen."

Kenji rolled his eyes. I saw Mrs. Karout smile a little. Jorge just looked puzzled.

"*Cual es tu nombre, mi amigo*?" said Kenji. He gently sat down on the bed next to the kid.

Jorge's eyes sparkled. A toothy grin transformed his face. He started rattling away in his native tongue.

"What's he saying?" I asked impatiently. Kenji just held up his hand, concentrating on Jorge's rapid-fire speech.

This went on for a few minutes. Finally, Jorge

seemed to talk himself out, and Kenji had a chance to ask some questions. Jorge answered these willingly enough, then went quiet. He was smiling. I saw that the milk glass wasn't trembling anymore.

"Well?" said X. "What's the 411?"

"His name's Jorge," began Kenji.

"We know that!" said Yusuf.

"Kenji, does he know where his parents are?" asked Mrs. Karout.

"That's the first thing I asked him," Kenji said. "He kept saying 'Ursula.' Anyone know what that means? Because I don't."

X spoke up. "It's the nickname of the biggest CBP detention facility in the country. It's on a street called Ursula Avenue down in Texas. It's in a town called McAllen, close to the border."

Kenji nodded. "McAllen. Yeah. I've heard of that place in the news. But Texas is a long way from Michigan."

"That makes our job harder," Mrs. Karout said. "But not impossible."

She put an arm around Jorge's bony shoulders and squeezed gently. He smiled. His milk glass was empty. Mrs. Karout looked around the room at us. "We will find this boy's family, and we will keep him safe. And, *in shaa Allah*, we will help this family come together again.

"The first thing, though, is to get Jorge to a safe place. There's a mosque in Detroit that we work with. They will shelter him until we can find a way to get his parents up here."

"Did he say why his family left El Salvador?" asked Yusuf.

Kenji spoke Spanish to Jorge, whose eyes immediately grew wide and fearful. He whispered two words so softly that we could barely hear him. "Mara Salvatrucha."

"Oh, man," said X. "That's what I was afraid of. Mara Salvatrucha is the worst gang in El Salvador. And that's saying a lot. His family must have gotten on their bad side. Not hard to do."

"You've done your homework," said Mrs. Karout.

"*Mataron a mi hermano Santiago*," whispered Jorge. "*Ellos lastimarán a mi papá si volvemos.*"

"Oh man," said Kenji.

"What'd he say?" I asked.

Kenji looked pale. "He said they killed his brother Santiago, and they'll hurt his dad if they go back."

We were silent for a moment. Then X spoke. "We have work to do, brothers. We gotta help these people."

He got no argument from any of us.

FIVE
Speak of the Devil

"I know just the guy."

This came from X's dad, Monty Maplethorpe, in his bullfrog croak. The big man sat in his usual spot in the Maplethorpe living room: a huge, old, cracked-red-leather easy chair. His bad leg was propped up on an equally old-looking red-leather ottoman. As usual, a cigar stuck out from one corner of his mouth. It filled the room with smoke. I tried not to inhale.

We all sat around the Maplethorpe living room. Plaques and medals hung on the walls—memorabilia from Detective Maplethorpe's impressive career. We wanted to hit the old man up for any info he could give us on the Ursula detention center.

"Bill Demaray," Monty continued, exhaling more smoke with each syllable. "He retired from the Detroit police department, is older than God himself, and knows everyone who is anyone in American law enforcement. He's got buddies in CBP, and he owes me a favor."

Monty grinned and chuckled. "A few months back, I backed him up when he told his old lady he'd been out fishin' with me. Really, he was at the casino. I probably saved ol' Billy's marriage, to tell you the truth."

"Yeah, cool, Pops," said X, one long leg bouncing up and down impatiently. "So, how can this dude help us?"

"His brother lives down in Texas—San Antonio— and works in CBP administration."

"Sweet!" I said. "Do you think his brother will hook us up with the info we need?"

"Don't know, Carlos," said Monty. "But like my Uncle Phil down in Mississippi always said, if you don't ask—"

"The answer is always no," finished X. His dad frowned at him. "Yeah, Pops, right on. But we gotta do something, and quick. This kid, Jorge Ramos, he's staying at Yusuf's right now. But customs is gonna come looking for him sooner or later. Word is they want to round up all the separated kids and put 'em with their families in detention. Family jail, in other words. Not cool."

"When I talk to Billy, we'll get the straight story from his brother in CBP," Monty said. He paused and stared at something through the big picture window in one wall of the living room. "Speak of the devil," he muttered.

We all turned to look. Outside, half a block down from the Maplethorpe house, a big white SUV rolled slowly down the street. I couldn't tell what make or model it was. It was too far away. But I could see the words "Customs and Border Protection" in huge letters across the SUV's rear window.

"This is not good, you guys," said Kenji in a low voice.

"Why are those guys here?" I asked nobody in particular.

Monty answered. "Lookin' for the kid," he said. "They probably knew he was stayin' at the church. When they went there and nobody was home, they decided to take a little spin around the hood. See if they could get lucky."

"But why now?" I said. "Why right after he ran to Yusuf's place?"

Monty shrugged. "Guess they want to hook him back up with his folks, like they're doing all over the country. Just a coincidence that they showed up right after he ran."

"Hook him up with his folks," snorted X. "Right. And throw the whole family in jail for who knows how long."

We watched the SUV pause at a stop sign three blocks down. Then it slowly turned and disappeared from view.

X looked at Yusuf, who was busy texting on his phone.

"Yo, Yusuf," said X. "We got a situation here, bro. Can't you hold off on that?"

Yusuf didn't answer at first. He was concentrating on whatever messages he was sending and receiving. Finally, he stuck the phone into a back pocket.

"I was texting my *yumma*," he said. "She—"

"Wait, your what?" said Monty, puffing out more clouds of foul smoke.

"His mom," said Kenji. "Anyway, Yusuf, you were warning your folks about the CBP, weren't you?"

Yusuf nodded. His big straw cowboy hat bobbed back and forth. "Yeah. But it turned out she already knew. I guess dad spotted them when he was saying afternoon prayers on our balcony. Speaking of..." He checked his watch. "Excuse me, everyone, it's time for *dhuhr*, the noon prayer. Detective Maplethorpe, is there a room I can use for a few minutes?"

"Sure, you can use the guest bedroom." He gestured down a short hallway off the living room. "Second door on your left."

"Thanks."

When Yusuf left, X spoke. "Jorge's in good hands, brothers. I don't think we need to worry about that for now. What we do need is to put our heads together on how we're gonna get Jorge's parents up here."

SIX
Dancing on the Roof

"We need to get back to Yusuf's place and check on Jorge," said Kenji worriedly. "That patrol was heading toward their building."

"They can't know he's there," I said. "How would they?"

"Who knows, man? Someone in the neighborhood who doesn't like people with dark skin probably called them."

"You guys get where you need to get," Monty said. "I'll get in touch with Billy Demaray and see what he can find out about the kid's parents. Go on, get." He waved at the front door with his cigar. Ash dropped to the floor.

A minute later, we all stepped out into the glaring summer sunlight. Heat rose from the sidewalk. Someone's dog slowly crossed the street on the next block, its tongue hanging out the side of its mouth. Even the trees looked listless and tired. Their leaves drooped in the still, hot air.

The only things that seemed happy about the weather were the cicadas. There seemed to be thousands of them, high up in the trees making their signature buzzing whine. Dozens of overlapping cicada calls cycled in volume from low to high and back to low again.

I shaded my eyes and looked around. I couldn't see the Border Patrol SUV anywhere.

We walked the short distance to Yusuf's building. When we came around a corner and into view of the small apartment block, my heart sank.

The big white SUV, which was a Ford Explorer with roof lights and reinforced front and rear bumpers, was parked at the curb in front of Yusuf's building. In a handicapped spot.

"We're too late," said Kenji.

"Nope," said X. "Look." He pointed to the side of the building, where unmowed grass and dandelions grew wild.

Making their way carefully through the weeds were two people in CBP uniforms, a man and a woman. The man was built like X, tall and lanky. The woman was shorter but even from a distance, I could tell she put in time at the gym. She was built like a wrestler, compact and muscular. They were searching the vicinity of the building before going inside.

"So what—" Kenji began, but he stopped when X suddenly broke into a run—straight toward the agents.

Or rather, toward their vehicle. He leaped up onto the enormous hood of the SUV, his sneakers coming down with a double whomp on the white sheet metal. My jaw dropped. All of us looked equally stunned.

But X wasn't finished. Another leap took him up onto the roof of the Explorer. Once there, he went into his best James Brown dance moves, flailing his long arms and bobbing his 'fro like a beach ball at a concert. He also started singing, wailing out the lyrics to "I Feel Good" at the top of his lungs.

All of this, of course, had the intended effect. Both agents whirled around and began shouting and running toward X. I stood frozen on the sidewalk. I was in awe of X's nerve and his apparent mental breakdown. Looking at the agents, I noticed that their uniform shirts were darkened by sweat stains. Sweat rolled freely down their faces.

"Walk, you guys! Walk," Yusuf whispered urgently.

Our little group was still where X had left us, maybe fifty feet from X's popup concert. I immediately realized what X was trying to do. Yusuf had figured it out a moment before me.

"Those officers don't know X is with us," I whispered. "He's distracting them. They won't even look at us with X making a scene like that."

The three of us started walking toward the apartment building, giving the SUV a wide berth. The agents had reached the car and were trying to haul X down from the roof. He kept dancing away from their hands, laughing like a maniac.

It was working. The agents paid no attention to us as we approached the building. A moment later, we strolled inside. We were just a small group of friends going to visit someone, or maybe binge watch something on Netflix. Nothing to see here, officers.

The small lobby was pleasantly cool and dim compared to outside. We quickly made our way up to Yusuf's place. He opened the door with his key. For the second time that day, we walked into the small, neat, well-decorated apartment.

SEVEN
We Need to Have a Few Words

"Yumma! Yabba!" Yusuf called.

"What is it, Yusuf?" This was Mrs. Karout's voice, coming from the kitchen. "Did you come in to escape the heat?"

We all trooped into the kitchen. Yusuf's parents were sitting at a small dining table with Jorge. The kid had showered and changed into a pair of dark-blue Rochester High School gym shorts that were

too big on him. He also wore a white Lipuma's Co-
ney Island T-shirt that was too small. But he was
grinning. He looked happy to see us. The three of
them were playing UNO.

"¡Hola!" said Jorge. "My... name... is... Jorge Ramos!" He looked proud.

"Nice," I said.

"We have to get him out of here," said Yusuf to
his parents. "CBP is right out front."

Mrs. Karout looked stricken. Mr. Karout's brow
furrowed with concern, but otherwise he didn't show
any reaction.

"Right now?" said Yusuf's mom.

Yusuf nodded. "Yeah, right now. We only got past
them because X distracted them."

I thought briefly about X and wondered what was
happening outside. Probably nothing good, I con-
cluded.

Jorge picked up on the sudden tension. His hun-
dred-watt smile faded. He looked at Kenji.

"¿Qué pasa?"

Kenji replied in Spanish. I didn't understand it,
but I could tell he was trying to reassure the kid.
I wasn't sure he had much success.

"Very well," said Mr. Karout calmly. He turned
to Yusuf's mom. "Fatme, we know what to do."

Mrs. Karout nodded and pulled her *hijab* more tightly around her head. Then she took Jorge's hand. "Kenji, can you translate, please?" she said.

"Of course, no problem."

"Thank you. Tell Jorge that we have to leave now, and that we are going to take him somewhere even safer than this apartment."

Kenji dutifully translated this into Spanish. Jorge looked scared, but he nodded.

Yusuf's father hugged the boy. Jorge stiffened at first, then returned the hug, wrapping his arms tightly around the man's neck.

"*Muchas gracias, señor*," he said against Mr. Karout's shoulder. Then he pulled away. Mrs. Karout took his hand, and they went to the front door of the apartment.

"I'll take him out the usual way," she said to her husband, who nodded. "Kenji, come with us, please, so you can translate."

"Sure," said Kenji. "No problem."

"We'll come too," I said. "People Movers stick together."

Just then there was a loud buzz from a small intercom mounted next to the door.

Mr. Karout pressed the TALK button on the intercom. "Yes, hello?" he said, putting his lips next to the speaker.

A female voice crackled out of the speaker, and it was a voice that meant business. "Customs and Border Patrol, sir. We need to have a few words with Mr. and Mrs. Karout."

EIGHT
Go!

"Go," said Mr. Karout.

We slipped single-file out the door with Mrs. Karout and Jorge in the lead. Kenji and Yusuf followed Jorge, I brought up the rear. As I passed by the intercom it crackled again, making me jump.

"Mr. Karout! Buzz us in immediately, or you'll be charged with obstruction," the voice said.

I had no idea if the agent was bluffing or if obstruction was actually something Yusuf's dad could be charged with. If it was a bluff, it was a good one. Mr. Karout closed the door as soon as I was out.

Out in the hallway, we could see the front stairs to our left. We headed to the right, toward the rear of the building. At the end of the corridor was a plain gray metal door with a worn brass handle. Mrs. Karout swung it open. We filed through.

I went last. Just before I closed the door behind us, I risked a glance back down the hallway... just in time to see the two border agents reach the top of the front stairs. I closed the door a second later, praying they hadn't noticed.

"Let's go," whispered Yusuf's mom. "Quickly."

We descended the steps, which were weakly lit by small, orange lamps set high on the concrete walls. After a minute, we reached the basement.

The stairs opened out onto a large, cobwebby, mostly empty space. The basement was punctuated every fifteen feet or so by thick, steel pillars. Weak sunlight filtered in through several small, grimy windows. The cinderblock walls were covered in peeling green paint that had faded to a drab olive color.

Clusters of water pipes, electrical conduits, and ventilation ducts snaked up the walls and out of sight through the ceiling. In one corner was a small pile of someone's long-forgotten laundry. The whole place smelled vaguely like a sweaty sneaker. A door in one wall had a cracked-plastic EXIT sign above it.

"This way," said Mrs. Karout.

Jorge, his hand still clutching Yusuf's mom's tightly, looked around silently. He was probably wondering where his life would take him next. If so, I couldn't blame him. So far his life had taken him from Central America to Texas to Rochester, Michigan.

Mrs. Karout reached the exit door first. She was about to push it open when a female voice yelled "Stop!" from the stairwell we had just descended. The command was amplified by the acoustics in the confined space.

We froze. Mrs. Karout had her hand on the door handle. Jorge's face was a mask of alarm. Mrs. Karout looked at him and silently raised a finger to her lips. He nodded, his eyes wide. The rest of us were as still as statues.

"Stay where you are, please. This is Customs and Border Patrol. We are coming down to you. We just need to ask you some questions."

They must have spotted us after all, I thought. *Uh-oh.*

I heard footsteps clattering down the stairs. The agents weren't visible yet, but they would be in a few seconds.

"Go!" whispered Yusuf urgently. "Everyone!

Quickly! Out!" He made a shoving gesture with his hands. The movement made his big straw cowboy hat fall to the floor.

Mrs. Karout didn't hesitate. She pushed the door open, letting a stream of sunlight and hot, humid air into the cool basement. She went out, pulling Jorge with her. Kenji followed.

I looked at Yusuf. The footsteps were louder. "What—?"

"Go!" he said, as loudly as he dared. This time, he didn't just pretend to shove. He put his palms against my shoulder blades and pushed me into the hot summer sun. Then he quickly closed the door behind me.

NINE
Saying the Asr

I'll tell you about what happened to Jorge, Mrs. Karout, Kenji, and me. But first, I'm going to fill you in on what Yusuf did after he pushed me out of that basement. I didn't learn about it until much later, after we all got back from Texas (don't worry, I'll tell you about that too). But it's a kick-butt part of this whole story. You need to hear it ASAP. Can you dig that?

Here's what happened:

Yusuf pushed me out the door and closed it just

seconds before the agents got to the basement. He was pretty sure they hadn't seen the door closing or heard the whispering. But it was really close.

Just as they came through the stairwell entrance, he grabbed an old towel from the pile of laundry in the corner. He spread it out on the floor. Then he knelt down on it and began praying aloud in Arabic.

("I started the *asr*, the afternoon prayer," Yusuf told me later. "So when they saw me, what they saw was a short Arabic kid kneeling on a towel, chanting, raising his hands up and down, putting his forehead to the floor, and raising it again. I think it kind of gave them the creeps.")

"Excuse us, young man," the short, muscular female agent said. "We need to ask you some questions." She didn't sound friendly. The male agent said nothing at this point.

Yusuf looked around at them in mock surprise. "Oh, I'm very sorry! I didn't hear you coming down the stairs. I'm saying *asr*, my afternoon prayer. Would you please wait until I'm finished? Then I'll be glad to help you."

Yusuf said all this in his most polite voice. It was the voice that invoked centuries of legendary Middle Eastern hospitality.

The agents looked more uncomfortable. They had obviously expected this teenage kid to comply.

But Yusuf just calmly went back to his prayer as if the agents didn't exist.

The woman spoke again. "Now. You can finish your asher or whatever it is later."

But Yusuf made no response. He just kept chanting.

It became clear that if the agents wanted to question Yusuf before he finished praying, they would have to actually lay hands on him. Yusuf later told me that the woman seemed more than willing to do that. But the man said, "We'll wait, Lieutenant Nelson. Let him finish. He isn't going anywhere."

"Captain, he's—" the woman began, then stopped.

This indicated to Yusuf that the man outranked her. He was thankful for this. If it had been the other way around, things would have gone much worse.

"We'll wait," said the man more sharply.

"Yes, sir," the woman said. She was clearly unhappy with the situation.

They retreated to the stairwell and sat down on the steps. Yusuf continued the asr, which lasted for several more minutes. He dragged it out by doing the chants especially slowly.

When asr was done, he moved into another set of ritual prayers. He was certain that the two agents wouldn't have a clue how long Muslim prayers typically lasted. And they didn't. They waited, and waited, and waited. Yusuf kept them waiting for a grand total of thirty minutes. After that long, even the captain seemed ready to grab Yusuf and haul him to his feet.

Finally, Yusuf finished and got to his feet. ("My legs were dead, Carlos! I couldn't feel them at all! I would have collapsed if the two border officers hadn't grabbed my arms.")

He went upstairs with Lieutenant Nelson and the captain, whose last name turned out to be Malley. They questioned Yusuf for about fifteen minutes with his dad present. They asked him about Jorge.

They asked if he knew who Jorge was, whether Jorge had been there, etc.

Yusuf asked them why the agents were talking to his family specifically, but he didn't get much of an answer. It didn't matter though. He'd succeeded where it counted. He gave the rest of us enough lead time to get away.

Which is exactly what we did. And that brings me back to what went down with the rest of us while Yusuf was literally praying for our safe escape.

TEN
Amigos

It took my eyes a few seconds to adjust to the dazzling sunlight. The heat was suffocating, but I barely noticed.

Behind the building was a small gravel parking lot. It was surrounded on three sides by tall, ivy-covered wood fences. A few cars were parked there. Mrs. Karout headed for a blue minivan with rust on the wheel wells and a large dent in the left rear fender. She took out her keys as we climbed inside. Mrs. Karout drove with Kenji riding shotgun and me and

Jorge on the bench seat right behind them.

I kept glancing back at the door we'd come through. I was worried that the border agents would come bursting through it and block our way out of the parking lot. But it didn't happen.

Yusuf's mom started the engine. It sputtered for a few seconds before catching and settling into a choppy idle. A minute later we drove through a narrow gate in one of the wood fences and turned onto Taylor Street. I watched the building recede as we drove away. I sent Yusuf and his dad all the good vibes I could muster.

Jorge was shaking a little bit. Kenji tried to calm him down in Spanish. It seemed to help, at least a little.

"Where are we headed?" Kenji asked Mrs. Karout.

"There's a mosque in downtown Detroit that takes in kids like Jorge," she said. She looked straight ahead as she drove through the Rochester traffic. "It's very close to the bridge into Canada.

"The imam at this mosque is a holy man. But he also knows that sometimes what is legal and what is right are two different things."

In a few minutes, we reached the entrance to the I-75. That was the main road to downtown Detroit from the northern suburbs. As we merged into the rush of traffic heading south, Jorge suddenly rattled off a long sentence in Spanish.

"What did he say?" I asked Kenji.

Kenji shook his head. "Not sure. He was talking too fast."

Kenji spoke to Jorge in Spanish. His tone and gestures told me he was telling Jorge to slow down and try again. The kid took a deep breath, then said the same thing more slowly.

"He says he was really scared those agents were going to get him," Kenji said.

"We will find your parents and bring them here," Mrs. Karout said firmly. "All three of you will get into Canada. You will be safe there."

Kenji translated all of this for Jorge. As the kid listened, I saw tears well up in his large brown eyes and spill onto his cheeks.

"*Gracias*," he said. "*Muchas gracias, mis amigos.*"

"You don't need to—" Kenji began, but he was interrupted. In the next instant, everything went horribly, horribly wrong.

ELEVEN
A Run for the Border

The next few seconds felt like an eternity. It felt like
I was inside a spinning dryer being jerked and tum-
bled and thrown around. I have a vague memory of
my head smacking into something hard.

I remember two things very clearly: I couldn't
hear any sound at all, and I clearly saw a small hand-
ful of coins. They probably fell out of a cupholder.
They seemed to float through the air as if they were
weightless. Those floating coins would appear in
my nightmares for years, long after the Ramos family

was gone and I stopped thinking about them.

Aside from the silence, the spinning, and the weightless coins, my first clear memory was of waking up in a hospital bed with X standing over me. I remember his Afro looking even bigger than usual because of how he was leaning over and looking into my face.

"Yo, C-man? You hearin' me, brother? You in there?"

At that moment, I knew two things. First, I had been in a car accident. Second, my head felt like someone was inside it swinging a mallet against the inside of my skull.

"What?" I began. My mouth was desert-dry. I decided questions could wait. "W-water?" I managed to croak.

"Yeah, baby!" said X. "Hey, Kenji! Carlos said 'water'! Get the man some water!"

A moment later a tall, plastic hospital cup swam into view. It had a straw poking out. I sucked at the straw and let me tell you, the water I drank right then was the sweetest stuff I had ever tasted. I finished it off and asked for more. After another half a cup, I felt ready to try speaking full sentences.

"What happened?" I said. I tried to sit up. The padded mallet in my head became a jackhammer. I collapsed back down to a flat position.

"No, no, brother, don't sit up," said X. "Doc says you need to lie down for a while."

I didn't need X or any doctor to tell me to lie flat. The guy in my head with the jackhammer was sending that message loud and clear.

"What happened?" I repeated, after the jackhammer had been replaced by the mallet again.

"A car accident," said another voice. Kenji's face joined X's hovering over me. He squinted through his thick glasses.

"Jorge—" I stopped when X and Kenji looked at each other in a way I didn't like.

"He's okay, C," said X. "Physically, anyway. But the CBP got him."

"How?" I asked, dismayed. "And what about Yusuf's mom? Is she okay? How'd they find us?"

Kenji said, "An ambulance came, and then a bunch of cops. A tire blew out on the minivan. We were going fifty miles an hour, and we rolled."

"That explains the whole dryer thing," I said to myself.

"What?" said Kenji.

"Never mind. I can't believe nobody got hurt worse." It was then that I realized something was wrapped around my head. I reached up and felt a gauze bandage. "What happened to my head?"

"Doc says you have a mild concussion," said X.

"You got off lucky, C-man. Real lucky."

"Nobody else got hurt? Nobody else on the road?"

Kenji shook his head. "Nope. We were in the right lane, and we rolled onto the shoulder. Landed upright too. Guess there really are such thing as miracles, huh?"

"Yeah," I said. It was a miracle I hadn't gotten my brains bashed in, for one. Then I remembered X's little escapade on the roof of the CBP vehicle. "Hey X, what happened after we went into Yusuf's building? Those agents arrested you, right?"

X laughed. "Nope. As soon as I saw you guys were inside, I jumped down and boogied out of there. They never had a chance. They didn't try too hard, though. Guess they cared more about rounding up the kid."

"Anyway," Kenji continued, "when the cops showed up at the scene of the accident, they recognized Jorge. I guess the border patrol must have put out some kind of bulletin on him for local law enforcement. They took him into custody with Yusuf's mom after the paramedics examined them. CBP showed up a few minutes later, and the cops handed them off."

He paused, staring at the floor. "Jorge was bawling. And I could tell Mrs. K wanted to also, but she put on a brave face. She told Jorge she'd come get him soon."

"Knuckleheads even put the little man in hand-cuffs," snorted X in disgust. "You believe that?"

"Where are they now?"

X answered. "Mrs. K is in the Wayne County jail since the accident and the arrest happened south of Eight Mile. My pops says he knows a lawyer that will spring her easy. They got nothing on her except for being in the same car with a little kid from Central America."

"But I guess maybe that's a crime in this country these days," I said.

X laughed a short, bitter laugh. It was unlike him. "No, it ain't, brother. No matter what some people want to think. You feel me?"

"I know, I know, man, chill," I said. "Where's Jorge?"

X and Kenji looked at each other again. I didn't like it one bit. That look told me loud and clear that I didn't want to hear the answer.

"He's on his way to Texas, Carlos," said Kenji. "CBP is transporting him down to McAllen where his parents are."

"How do you know all that?" I asked. I looked at X. "Ah, your dad."

X nodded. "Right on. Pops talked to that dude,

Bill Demaray, who talked to his contacts at CBP. It was all back-channel-type stuff. Off the record. Little Jorge might be on an airplane right now. They expedited his transport 'cause of the deadline to reunify the families."

X was talking about a court-ordered date by which all separated kids were supposed to be reunited with their parents. I was glad that, at least, they were doing something. But it made me sick to think the whole disaster could have been avoided in the first place.

"And when they get Jorge back with his folks..." I began, then trailed off, not wanting to say it aloud.

"Yeah," said Kenji. "Back to El Salvador."

"Where Mara Salvatrucha will be waiting for them," I said grimly, remembering the footage we'd seen on YouTube. "Fellas, we gotta do something. We gotta help that family, no matter where they are."

Suddenly X and Kenji both smiled. I realized why when X held up five sheets of paper. They each had the American Airlines logo on them.

"Four round trip tickets to McAllen, Texas," he said, waving the papers in front of me. "My brother, the People Movers are makin' a run for the border!"

"We're going to Texas?" I said. "When? And what are we going to do when we get there?"

"Day after tomorrow," X said proudly. "What

we're gonna do is play a gig at the detention center. Like Johnny Cash at Folsom Prison back in the day."

"And how'd you pull that off?" I said. "Wait, don't tell me. Your dad's buddy, Bill Demaray."

X nodded. "He owes my pops a favor. Turns out the director of Ursula owed him a favor too. Guy named Franks. Something about liquor smuggling and a bench warrant from twenty years ago.

"This Franks dude thought that ordeal was dead and buried. Lucky for us, Demaray unburied it."

"Okay, we play a show for the people stuck in Ursula," I said. "I'm totally down for that. But how does it help Jorge and his parents?"

"That's the best part," said X.

Then he told me his plan. It confirmed my suspicion that my lead singer was the craziest dude in Michigan, if not the country. But if it worked, it would be the best jailbreak since the Birdman of Alcatraz.

TWELVE
Deep in the Heart of Texas

Texas is hot in the summer. I mean, really hot. As in I-fell-asleep-and-woke-up-in-a-pizza-oven hot.

The heat is the first thing that hit me as I stepped off the plane. It was a small, twin-prop commuter plane that had taken us from our connection at Dallas/Fort Worth down to McAllen. McAllen was a small city just a few miles from the Mexico border.

Coming out of the door at the top of the stairway, I immediately broke out in a sweat. My head, which hadn't hurt in the two days since I'd been released from the hospital, began to ache. I prayed my new nemesis, the jackhammer, wouldn't come back. This trip was too important.

My bandmates and I descended the stairs and walked across the blazing tarmac. A hot, dry wind blew dust in our faces. We made it into the terminal, where it was blessedly cool. Then we found the Avis car rental counter.

X had reserved a Ford Econoline cargo van. We got in and drove around to the freight terminal, where a ground-crew member helped us load our gear. X had used the proceeds from our last few gigs to buy heavy-duty rolling crates like the ones professional bands use on tour. There were three empty crates, too, big ones. Those were an essential part of our rescue plan.

With the van fully loaded and X driving, we left the airport. We soon entered a wasteland of industrial properties and vacant lots. Palm trees were scattered here and there like forgotten ornaments. The only other vegetation were scrubby bushes and thickets of vines clustered around rusting chain-link fences.

The sheet-metal warehouse buildings were streaked with rust. Between buildings, I caught sight of what looked like endless, flat fields. They were pale green and light brown. I couldn't tell if they were farms or just big abandoned lots. A faint chemical smell hung in the air.

The detention center was only a couple of miles from the airport. When we arrived, we pulled up across the street from the main gate to have a quick look at the place.

It buzzed with activity. We couldn't see much of the building itself because it was surrounded by tall chain-link fencing. Brown plastic was woven into the links to keep people like us from seeing through it.

An endless parade of vehicles passed in and out of the single visible gate in the fence. There were many Customs and Border Protection SUVs like the one we'd seen in Michigan, as well as civilian cars and large delivery trucks.

As we watched, a white bus with the letters "CBP" stenciled in black along the side pulled up to the gate. The gate opened to let the vehicle through. I saw small faces pressed up against the bus's windows. Their eyes were wide with curiosity, fear, or both.

"That bus has kids on it," said Kenji. He was sitting next to me in the back seat. I nodded, wondering when those kids had seen their parents last. And when, or if, they would see them again.

"Let's get inside," said X.

We pulled up to the gate. There was an intercom box on a post. X pushed the CALL button. A toneless male voice asked us who we were. A closed-circuit television camera, perched high on the post over the gate, peered down at us. I resisted the urge to wave.

"We're the People Movers, my man!" said X. "Director Franks is expecting us."

The toneless voice didn't answer. The gate didn't move. We waited. A minute went by, then two.

I was just beginning to wonder what kind of prison sentence we'd get if we rammed the van through the gate when it slid open.

"See? No worries, fellas," said X as we drove through. But he sounded relieved.

✷ ✷ ✷

When we walked into the Ursula detention center, escorted by Director Bryan Franks and three uniformed officers, my first impression was that it looked like a giant dog kennel built inside a gym. There were two reasons for this.

First, the chain-link fencing dominated the massive open space.

The fencing divided most of the space up into what Franks described as "pods." I thought they looked more like cages. Each one was maybe twenty feet wide. Double rows of cages were separated by aisleways. Each cage had a small gate that opened onto the aisleway alongside it.

Second, it was loud in there. I estimated that there were at least three hundred people divided up among the cages. Each cage held at least three people. The background din of hundreds of voices all talking at once echoed around the cavernous room.

Most of the cages seemed to be occupied by parents with one or more child ranging in age from toddler to teen. With a growing sense of dread, I noticed that some of the cages contained only kids.

Those must be the kids taken from their parents at the border, I thought.

I glanced at my bandmates. By the looks on their faces, I could tell they felt the same sinking feeling. One nearby cage contained four kids and no adults. In it was a skinny, dark-haired boy. He couldn't have been older than six. He was changing the diaper of a toddler-age girl. The girl was lying on a thin mattress on the concrete floor of the cage, wailing.

Another kid in the same cage was curled up in a fetal ball in a corner. Her face was buried in her hands. An older girl was talking to the balled-up kid and pulling gently at her arms, trying to get her to sit up and talk.

"This place..." said Yusuf. He spoke so softly

I could hardly hear him even though he was right next to me. "This place is *la 'insani*. Soulless."

I glanced at him. He was crying. *La 'insani*. Soulless. It described the Ursula facility perfectly.

"Stay strong, my brothers," murmured X as Director Franks led us past the cages. "Remember, we're gonna turn this place into Funk Central." But I could tell he was as upset as the rest of us.

Franks took us to a large open area at one end of the room. A small stage had been set up against a wall.

"This is where you'll play," said Franks. He didn't look happy about having to host a concert in his facility. His tone said, *Watch your step, or you're out of here*. "Hope it's big enough."

"This will be great," said X in his best spread-the-love voice. "Thank you, director. Big, big props."

Franks glowered at X, who smiled right back.

"Let's get our stuff in here," said Kenji.

Twenty minutes later, with the help of a couple of CBP agents (who were friendlier than their boss), everything was inside and uncrated. Everyone in the place watched us as we set up amps and pluged in cables.

Yusuf's kit, as usual, took the longest. We all pitched in with that.

By the time we were done, the whole place

seemed to be talking about us in English and Spanish. Kenji told me that most of the kids he overheard kept saying, "They're going to play music!"

During our setup, I kept looking around for some sign of Jorge. I didn't see him, but there were so many kids there that this didn't mean much. I asked my bandmates if they'd spotted him.

They shook their heads.

"What if they've already been deported?" said Kenji, looking worried. "They might be gone already. How will we know?"

"Dude, we're here now," I said as I tightened a crash cymbal onto its stand. "What are we gonna do, pack up and leave?"

"I'm just saying..."

"Look, I hear you, Kenji," I said. "It would be legit bad news if the Ramoses weren't here. But X's dad said his info was solid. So let's roll with it."

Kenji nodded but continued to scan the vast space.

"You guys ready?" said Franks, walking up to X.

"Yes, sir," X replied. "When do we start?"

"Fifteen minutes." Then he turned and walked away.

"That guy is way too uptight," said X. "Hey, C-man, help me move those crates, will you?"

X and I moved the three largest crates up against

the wall at the back of the stage.

A man in gray custodian's coveralls approached us. "I need one of you guys to help me bring some chairs down here."

"Got it covered," I said.

I jumped off the stage and followed the custodian to the far end of the room. I listened to the cacophony of voices echoing off the sheet-metal walls and high ceiling. Finally we reached a flatbed cart piled with metal folding chairs.

"Gimme a hand," said the custodian. He grabbed the raised metal bar on one end of the cart that served as a handle. I stood next to him and grasped the cold metal.

Then I saw them.

Right there, less that ten feet from me, inside a chain-link cage, was the Ramos family.

THIRTEEN
Showtime

Jorge and his parents were sitting on air mattresses on the floor. They were playing some kind of card game. Jorge happened to look up at me almost as soon as I saw him. His face lit up like a Christmas tree. He jumped up, dropping his cards and running up to the fence.

His father was a tired-looking bald man with a big black moustache. His mother was an even more exhausted looking woman. Her long, dark hair was tied back in a disheveled ponytail. She gaped at their son.

"Carlos! Carlos! *¡Mi amigo!*" Jorge grabbed the fence and rattled it. The entire wall of the cage shook and jingled, drawing looks from a couple of nearby CBP officers.

"Hey, little man!" I said, a big goofy grin spreading over my face. "*¿Que pasa?*"

Then he started speaking in Spanish. I had no hope of understanding. I just smiled and spread my hands: *I don't understand.*

"You know that kid?" said the custodian.

It occurred to me that it probably wasn't a good idea to attract attention. I just nodded and began pushing, hoping the guy wouldn't ask any more questions. He didn't, and we were back at the stage in a couple of minutes. I drew the others aside on the pretense of checking some cable connections. I quickly told them about the Ramoses.

"Right on!" whispered X. "Don't know about you fellas, but that's a load off my mind."

"I'll go tell them what they need to do," said Kenji. He jogged off.

Showtime.

We were all in our places: Yusuf behind his kit, Kenji with his guitar on stage left, and me with mine on stage right. As always, X was front and center. His huge Afro bobbed as he nodded and waved to the crowd.

And it was a crowd Every one of those hundred chairs was filled.

People stood two rows deep around the back and sides of the chairs. The cages were mostly emp-ty. Around the perimeter of the performance area was a ring of officers standing shoulder to shoulder.

This will never work, I thought. But it has to.

"How y'all doin'?" X shouted into his mic.

His voice boomed through the detention facili-ty. And I didn't know how many of the immigrants in the crowd understood him, but they heard him. They responded with a hearty roar. Several kids in front jumped up and down with excitement.

Off to my right, at the edge of the crowd and right up against the stage, were Jorge and his par-ents. The grownups looked anxious, knowing full well what they would need to do soon.

Jorge, however, looked transported with joy. He was looking right at me. He gave me two big thumbs up. I pointed at him and blasted out a power E-chord on my Fender, hitting my effects pedal to give it plenty of crunch. That caused Jorge, and most of the crowd, to scream and whoop.

"Awww, yeah. I think y'all are doin' pretty GOOD!!" said X. "We know you've traveled many miles, gone hungry, and overcome the worst odds to find a better life for yourselves. The People Movers give all of you BIG props! Thank you so much for gathering 'round to listen to our tunes, dig our magic, and most of all FEEL THE LOVE, BABY!!"

That was our cue. I dug into the opening riff of "Play That Funky Music" by Wild Cherry. It was a crowd pleaser. Yusuf and Kenji joined in a minute later. When X added his banshee wails over our instrumentation, it was all over.

That crowd might not have understood the lyrics, but they felt every word and every note. And we felt them. The energy was off the charts. A happy electricity filled the air in the Ursula detention facility that hot Texas afternoon. To this day, the People Movers have never played a better show.

But the big finish, the literal showstopper, was the best part. Here's what went down...

FOURTEEN
For Those
About to Rock

The scene inside the detention center during our last tune reminded me of our St. Andrews show: loud and crazy. The CBP officers posted around the crowd had their work cut out for them trying to keep everyone inside the perimeter. Director Franks observed everything from a small, glassed-in office that contained a bunch of TV screens. He wore a scowl that could have withered a cactus.

The kids danced in front of the stage. The grownups watched from a little further back (and a few of them danced too). I even caught a few of the officers grooving a little.

X was in top form, strutting around the stage like a cross between James Brown and Mick Jagger. Kenji stayed rooted to his part of the platform, fingers flying over his Fender Jazz bass. Yusuf gave his kit the workout of a lifetime. His beats thundered through the huge room and sweat poured down his face. I lit the room on fire with some of my best solo work. At one point I even did some Eddie Van Halen neck-hammering with the fingers of my strumming hand.

Most importantly, the Ramos family were gradually edging around the front-right corner of the stage. From there, they were to move along the edge of the platform toward the three big crates.

Our final number was AC/DC's "For Those About To Rock." We don't normally do heavy metal stuff, but the recorded version of the song has cannons firing. What could be better for a dramatic rescue?

X got the crowd whipped up as he screamed out the words to one of rock's greatest anthems. I jumped and whirled and kicked like a madman as I blasted out hair-raising power chords. Yusuf was a blur behind me. Even Kenji, Mister Calm and Collected, started busting some moves.

Finally, the big finale of the song came. X belted out "For those about to rock!" We all screeched to a halt, leaving a sudden sonic gap, a silence that was deafening. In the recording, that's when the first cannon shot comes. For us, it was our cue to execute the plan.

I didn't actually see Yusuf step on the trigger pedal for the flashpot hidden against the wall behind his kit. But I knew he had done it when there was a deafening bang and a spout of flame shot up behind the crates.

Then there was smoke. It quickly enveloped the crates, the stage, and the crowd. It was so thick that I couldn't see anyone. All I heard was a lot of confused yelling in English and Spanish. I dropped to the stage and lay flat, squeezing my eyes shut and praying this stunt would be worth it.

After a couple of minutes, the smoke had cleared enough to let me get over to the edge of stage right. That's where the Ramoses had been waiting for the flashpot to go off—their cue to make themselves scarce. The three big crates stood where we'd left them. But Jorge and his parents were gone.

"Dudes, I think it worked!" I said as the rest of the band came over to join me.

"It did," said Yusuf, smiling. "It almost killed me,

but it worked."

"Unbelievable," said Kenji. "Freaking unbelievable."

"Naw, bass man, not unbelievable at all," said X. He winked at us. "Let's get these crates loaded in the van, double time, before—"

Director Franks's voice boomed out over a PA system.

"All detainees return to your pods immediately! All detainees return to your pods immediately! There will be a head count in five minutes!"

"Before that head count happens," finished X.

Director Bryan Franks was, in a word, pissed.

He emerged from his glass office a moment after broadcasting his order. He stormed over to where we were wheeling the big crates toward the exit. Then he gave us a piece of his mind.

I'll leave his exact words to your imagination. It was some salty language, though. I think he used every four-letter word in the book, and a few I'd never heard before. But his gist was clear: Pack up your stuff and get out of my facility before I have all of you arrested.

We didn't need to be told twice. Under Franks's watchful eye, we carefully loaded the three crates into the van. We got the rest of our gear stashed into the van in record time. We didn't even bother to break down Yusuf's kit. Somehow we found space for each drum, cymbal, stand, and pedal among the rest of the equipment.

I closed the rear doors. We piled in and pulled up to the gate. Franks signaled to the camera and the gate opened. We rolled out, Franks still staring after us with an angry scowl.

We would never see Ursula again.

FIFTEEN
I Hate Basketball

It turned out, though, that Ursula wasn't quite done with us yet.

About ten minutes after we arrived at the airport, a CBP car came screaming into the lot. It had its flashers and sirens on full blast. None of us were surprised that our little ruse hadn't gotten us very far. We stood and waited as the car stopped next to us and four officers got out.

One of them, of course, was Director Franks. He walked up to X and got right into his face.

"You really thought you and your little kiddie band would get away with it, didn't you?" he yelled, spit flying.

X was calm. "We ain't no kiddie band, bro. Show some respect."

This made Franks go from red to purple. "You ever been to juvenile detention, kid?" he shouted, more at X's chin than anything else. X had at least four inches on the man. Then he looked at X's huge Afro. "And what kind of hair is that, by the way? You think you're Kareem Abdul Jabbar or something?"

"I hate basketball," X replied.

Franks ignored this. "Open these crates," he ordered the other officers. "Those first." He pointed to the three big ones, which sat on the tarmac a few feet away.

"Yes, sir," one of them said. He was a young guy with sandy-blond hair and a surfer tan. He quickly unlatched the door to the biggest crate. Franks and the two remaining officers had their hands on their gun butts.

"Come out of there!" shouted Franks as the surfer dude swung the crate door open.

SIXTEEN
Miles Away

The crate was empty.

Franks and his men were dumbstruck for a good five seconds. Then he ordered the other two opened. They were as empty as the first.

"Search this vehicle!" he shouted.

"Hold on," said Kenji. "You don't have a warrant. And you aren't going to find... whatever you're looking for, anyway. By the way, what are you looking for?"

"Quiet," Franks snapped.

I'd never seen a person so furious. Ever heard the phrase "thunderclouds gathered on his brow"? Director Franks's face seemed to have an entire hurricane sitting on it. He and his officers searched the rest of our stuff, even though none of the other crates and boxes were big enough to hold a person.

After ten minutes, everything we'd brought was strewn across the asphalt of the freight loading dock. I managed to rescue my Strat and Kenji's Jazz bass from rough handling, but everything else sustained some dents and scratches.

Finally, Franks seemed to realize that the Ramos family wasn't folded up and stuffed into any of our boxes. He glared at us and opened his mouth as if to say something. Then he snapped it closed, turned, and stalked off to the CBP truck.

The other three officers followed him. The surfer dude caught my eye as he passed and whispered, "Nice guitars, dude!" Before I could respond, he and the rest of them got back into their car. Then they rolled out of the parking lot and were gone.

"Think they got far enough?" I said to nobody in particular.

X nodded. "Think so. My pops called in another favor down here. There was a car waiting for them outside."

"Say what? Who—"

X shook his head. "I don't know. Pops wouldn't tell me. He just said there's some things I'm better off not knowing."

"So they're miles away already," said Yusuf.

"Right on," said X. "They're gonna drive to an airstrip out in the sticks, then a pilot's gonna fly 'em up to Michigan. They'll be up there before we will."

"I can hardly believe it," Kenji said, shaking his head. "We actually pulled it off. X, you're either insane or a certified genius."

"We all did it, brothers. We rocked the house and gave those people in there something to be happy about. Even if we hadn't gotten the Ramoses out, it still would've been worth it. Am I right?"

He got no argument from any of us.

EPILOGUE
Oh, Canada!

Six hours later, we were back in Rochester. After stashing the equipment in my garage, we went straight to Yusuf's apartment.

"Come in!" said Mrs. Karout when she opened the door. She swept each of us into a tight embrace as soon as we entered.

"We are so glad you're all back safely," said Mr. Karout.

Then we saw the Ramoses.

They came out from the back bedroom, looking tired but happy.

Jorge's mother, Flores, began weeping and speaking in Spanish. Kenji translated it as a series of thank you's. Jorge climbed up on X, who held the kid in the crook of one bony arm while Jorge played with his Afro.

"Yeah, little man. You wanna have cool hair like me someday, don't you?" said X.

We learned that all three of them were fine except for a nasty scratch on Jorge's back. It had been acquired as he and his parents crawled out through the hole in the wall behind the stage—the hole made by the flashpot's discharge.

How did a theater pyrotechnic gizmo manage to cut through sheet metal? You guessed it: magnesium. X had laced the flashpot's charge with the stuff, leftovers from his garage demonstration. We'd placed the device under the stage below Yusuf and pointed it at the wall. The Ramoses had crawled behind the stage under cover of the smoke. Then they escaped through the hole cut open by the magnesium's white-hot flame.

So yeah, now you know why we all thought X was insane. We still do, actually.

We also learned that the Ramoses were due to leave for Canada in an hour. I was glad we'd made it back in time to see them.

Jorge's father, Juan-Miguel, was a lawyer. Once

the family was established in Canada, he planned to help the Karouts ferry more refugee families over the border and get them legal status in America's more welcoming northern neighbor. Flores, it turned out, was a teacher and planned to organize a small school for refugee kids.

Jorge told us he wanted to grow up to be a famous guitarist. He earned a big high five from me on that one.

The Ramoses made it into Canada without incident. The busiest border crossing in the world had its advantages. It was relatively easy to get through customs on the Canadian side. Then they could apply for asylum. Unlike the United States, Canada didn't jail refugees just for wanting to escape persecution.

They wound up settling in Windsor, right across the river from Detroit. From there they could look at the country that had tried to hold them captive and know that they were safe.

Juan-Miguel's law practice flourished, as did Flores's school.

Jorge did learn to play the guitar, although when he discovered math in middle school, he fell in love. The six-string ended up taking a back seat to numbers. The kid turned out to be a prodigy. By ninth grade, he'd mastered advanced calculus and was already being courted by major universities.

So everything turned out all right for the Ramoses. You feel me?

I didn't like to think about all the other people stuck in that big dog kennel in Texas and all the other places like it around the country.

But at least we'd done something. And I kept up the hope that people like Jorge, Juan-Miguel, and Flores, who just wanted to be safe, would eventually be welcome in my country. When that happened, America really would be great again.

About the Author

Brian lives in southeastern Michigan with his wife and three kids. He is a college administrator and professor of geological sciences by day, writer and guitarist by night. He is the Grand Prize winner of the 2016 Relevant Reads Contest.

About the Publisher

Storyshares is a publisher focused on supporting the millions of teens and adults who struggle with reading by creating a new shelf in the library specifically for them. The ever-growing collection features content that is compelling and culturally relevant for teens and adults, yet still readable at a range of lower reading levels.

Storyshares generates content by engaging deeply with writers, bringing together a community to create this new kind of book. With more intriguing and approachable stories to choose from, the teens and adults who have fallen behind are improving their skills and beginning to discover the joy of reading.

For more information, visit storyshares.org.

Easy to Read. Hard to Put Down.